REBECCA
and the
Strangest Garden

by

V. V. Thomas

Originally published on Amazon Kindle by V. V. Thomas under the pen name of Imogen Daley

First published in paperback in Great Britain in 2016 by Thomas V Publishing

Thomas V Publishing
PO Box 43278, Hanwell, London, W7 3XR
www.thomasvpublishing.com

Illustrations by Argha Mondal
Illustrations © V. V. Thomas and Argha Mondal 2016
Cover design by HaVaa (vasdevrao@gmail.com)
Typeset and designed by
Berean Services UK (bereanservicesuk@gmail.com)

A catalogue record for this book is available from the British Library.

Paperback ISBN: 978-1-911050-02-5

Printed and bound in Great Britain by Clays Ltd.

CONTENTS

This book is dedicated to
Minette
my dear Mother
who is always kind to plants

Special thanks to
Jackie Raymond
of Berean Services UK

Chapter One
A CRY FOR HELP

"Rebecca!!!" called Auntie Sue. "It's time to do your homework!"

Rebecca hurriedly changed out of her school uniform and into her shorts and T-shirt. She always enjoyed her visits to Auntie Sue's, as she was lovely and very playful for an auntie. She would cook the most delicious meals, and sing and dance around her house as though she were a little schoolgirl.

Auntie Sue always had little treats up her sleeve for Rebecca. Even more than that, she had a special love for her garden. She cared for it regularly, and Rebecca always heard Auntie Sue speaking very tenderly to her many plants.

Rebecca really loved wandering

around the garden, examining the plants and flowers. There were red petals, white blossoms, lilac, orange, different shades of blue...

Auntie Sue would say, "Speak nicely to the plants, and they will be sure to grow and blossom. Look after them well, and they will look after you!" Rebecca never could understand what she meant, but she always marvelled at the amount of time Auntie Sue spent with them, and they always looked colourful and beautiful. Yes, Rebecca was looking forward to spending this half term week at Auntie Sue's.

"I promised your Mother that you would do your homework before supper," she said, pouring herself and Rebecca a large glass of elderflower water, with ice balls floating on the surface.

"Auntie..." Rebecca began, reaching for her glass and a big slice of chocolate cake, "…please may I do my homework in the garden?" she asked, half hoping that it would give her an opportunity to skive. How she hated her maths.

Auntie Sue glanced out through the window. It was a hot summer's afternoon, and there was a mild breeze blowing through the leaves of the apple blossom tree. She could well understand why any youngster full of life and energy wouldn't want to be locked up inside. Outside, the birds, bees and flowers seemed to stare invitingly at them both …

"Of course you may," she replied. "I've still got a lot of housework to do. Give me a shout if you need any help."

Rebecca grabbed her pencil, maths book, cake and drink and ran outside. Placing her book, pencil and glass of elderflower water on the bench, she set to work, munching on her chocolate slice, which she soon finished. In the distance, she could hear Auntie Sue singing very loudly, "O happy day, O happy day, when He washed my sins awaaaay..."

Rebecca felt happy with the plan for the afternoon: homework, play, supper and then bed. She was looking forward to dining with her auntie. Once again, she had cooked Rebecca's favourite meal: jerk chicken, rice and green salad. Vanilla ice cream with raspberry sauce was sure to follow, but before that... Rebecca reluctantly glanced down at her homework.

"One hundred and forty-seven minus eighty-nine..." Oh dear, Rebecca hated maths. She found it difficult and boring. But Auntie Sue had said, "Nothing is more important than knowing how to count. Never rely on calculators and computers; we should all know simple maths!"

This, however, did not seem like 'simple maths' to Rebecca. She liked spelling, but not this.

As she struggled to find the answer, she was interrupted by a rather strange voice calling her, "Rebecca! Rebecca!"

Rebecca rose to her feet and

looked around. "Who is it?" she asked. "Who's there?" She glanced quickly around the garden, but couldn't see anybody.

"It's Miss Bateman," the voice replied. "I'm so sorry to distract you from your homework."

"Who are you, and where are you?" Rebecca asked, slightly curious to find out where the voice could possibly be coming from. It was a very gentle and friendly voice, so Rebecca was not in the slightest bit afraid.

"I'm just in front of you," replied Miss Bateman.

"I beg your pardon?" Rebecca exclaimed. *Surely not*, she thought, as there was nothing around except the plants and flowers. "What do you look like?"

"Well, my dear," Miss Bateman continued, "I'm wearing my white suit and my red top." Miss Bateman was enjoying this little game, knowing that Rebecca was more than slightly confused.

Rebecca gasped as she realised that Miss Bateman was none other than the clematis plant Auntie Sue had planted a few summers ago. Rebecca had always looked forward to when it blossomed into white flowers with red centres.

"What, do you mean...?" Rebecca asked, incredulously. "Plants can't talk!"

"But of course we can, dear!" Miss Bateman chuckled at Rebecca's bewilderment. "Your Auntie Sue spends hours talking away to us, but she never stops to listen to what we have to say."

"We?" asked Rebecca. "What do you mean, 'we'?"

"Oh, the other plants speak too, you know. Normally they elect me to make the first introduction, because they think I'm bolder and wiser than they are," Miss Bateman continued.

"Well, you sure are colourful," enthused Rebecca, "and you do brighten up the fence very well."

"That is so kind of you," responded Miss Bateman, before swaying to avoid the buzzing bees that had just appeared to settle onto her red centres. How she disliked their intrusion!

"The matter at hand! The matter at hand!" boomed a loud, impatient and very cantankerous voice.

"Who is *that*?" asked Rebecca, startled at the interruption, and beginning to feel a little uneasy.

"Oh, that's the President," replied Miss Bateman. "He's my cousin, but he's very bossy, really..." she added with a whisper.

Rebecca looked behind and saw another clematis plant with bold, violet flowers.

"We are being invaded... an enemy attack is looming!" he continued, with the same sense of urgency. "We must take action!"

"What on earth is he talking about?" Rebecca was starting to feel nervous at the thought of some invisible enemy invading Auntie Sue's garden.

"Well, I was nominated to request your assistance in an urgent matter," explained Miss Bateman, "which is why I called you earlier. Some very small but vicious enemies are invading us, and they are destroying us at our very roots. Auntie Sue is so happy with the blooms and the colours in the garden every year, that she forgets to inspect us properly, and we won't be here next year if she doesn't do something quickly!"

"Enemy activity is threatening the very foundations and security of our nation..." rumbled the President.

"Strong retaliatory action is required!"

"But what can *I* do to help?" asked Rebecca.

"Look carefully under my white blossom, at the leaves," Miss Bateman instructed. "There you'll find proof."

As Rebecca gently pulled back the white petals, she was shocked to find that Miss Bateman's leaves had small nibble marks, which were barely visible to the naked eye.

"You must tell Auntie Sue!" pleaded Miss Bateman desperately. She was aware of the look of surprise etched onto Rebecca's young face. "Tell her *today*, so that she can take action *immediately*."

"Our very survival depends on it!" echoed the President.

*"Would you like me to give you
a drink now?"*

Chapter Two
DANGER IN THE GARDEN

Rebecca couldn't imagine a summer without the beautiful, colourful flowers strewn throughout the garden. She often found the garden a place of refuge, where she could escape whenever she wanted peace and quiet. She often liked to sit, draw or paint with the familiar sound of the birds singing and the bees humming in the background.

"I am so sorry that this is happening to you," she said, deep in thought about what it could mean.

"I *will* tell Auntie Sue, and I'll show her the nibbles on your leaves," she promised.

"You must, my dear," Miss Bateman stressed. "Just look at the plants opposite us. They have stopped speaking altogether now. It's to do with enemy invasion, lack of proper food and bad air."

Lack of proper food? Bad air? Never before had Rebecca thought of plants and flowers not eating or breathing properly.

She turned to look at the flowers and plants on the opposite wall. Funnily enough, she had never felt drawn to any of those; they always seemed duller and less inviting than her new friends.

"Pollution," explained Miss Bateman. "It's particularly worse at that end of the garden." It was as though she knew exactly what Rebecca was thinking. "Also, last year

Auntie Sue held a barbecue, which so choked and smothered them that they've never been the same since."

Rebecca was becoming more intrigued by the plants, the garden, and the talk of invading armies. She didn't quite know what to make of it all. Maybe she was just very tired, and had imagined the whole thing. Maybe the sun was far too hot for her, and she needed an afternoon nap. She dragged the bench closer to the fence, into the shade, and tried to continue with her homework.

I think I'll just forget the whole thing, she thought, even though she couldn't easily forget the nibbles on Miss Bateman's leaves, or the dull flowers on the opposite wall. More importantly, there was the chance that they wouldn't be there next summer if she didn't take action. *I'll ask Mum to help me look it up on the computer when I get home,* she decided. *Mum always seems to find answers on there. I wonder if she could find out about plants that can talk, or about invading armies...?*

"Fifty-eight!" called the President, as Rebecca tried to concentrate on her homework. "We've conferred, and my final decision is that the answer is fifty-eight."

"Pardon?" asked Rebecca. She had no idea what the President was referring to this time, and looked at Miss Bateman for clarification.

"He's talking about your homework, dear. You know: 'one hundred and forty-seven minus eighty-nine'. He is trying to help you, dear, and says the answer is fifty-eight. He's good like that, you know," Miss Bateman said to reassure her, "and he likes to have the last word, too," she added in a whisper.

"Do you *all* speak?" asked Rebecca. She felt sure that this wasn't her imagination after all.

"Well, it all depends on the weather, you see, and the time of year." Miss Bateman was being very patient and gentle with Rebecca. "We prefer the sunshine, and without it we're so tired. If we get too thirsty or hungry, we'll be too parched to say even one syllable!"

"Wow!" exclaimed Rebecca. She had never considered that plants and flowers, like herself, felt happier and more content when the sun was out, and if they were well fed and watered. "Would you like me to give you a drink now?" she offered, reaching for her elderflower water.

"Goodness, no – not yet, dear!" Miss Bateman hurriedly replied, thinking of her roots being clogged up by the thick syrupy fluid in the transparent container. No, it was sufficient for her to have to contend with the invading pests, let alone to have this added to her fate!

"There are many of us here," she continued, in a vain attempt to distract Rebecca from pouring elderflower water onto her soil. "Would you like me to introduce you to everyone?"

"Oh, yes, please!" beamed Rebecca.

Chapter Three
REBECCA'S NEW FRIENDS

Miss Bateman uttered a slight cough-like sound, as if clearing her throat. With an animated voice, trying to sound very formal (but which actually sounded really funny), she proceeded with the introductions.

Rebecca found this quite entertaining; she couldn't believe that plants could even speak, let alone have a sense of humour. They had always looked stern yet serene in their various colours and shades.

She decided there and then to

make a New Year's resolution: work hard in the garden and develop green fingers. She reasoned that this would be a better resolution than having to give up chocolate.

"I would like to introduce you to my cousin, the President," Miss Bateman began, in her hoity-toity voice, "whom you have already met."

"Ever so nice to meet you," came the recognisable voice that had so startled Rebecca earlier with the talk of 'enemy activity' and the like.

Rebecca looked towards the deeper, velvety voice, and was in awe of the vibrant purple colour around his leaves. She had been too shy to examine them earlier, but now she admired their colour and grandeur. His name, however, was a mystery.

Why was he called 'the President'? What exactly did he preside over, here in the garden? Rebecca wondered. He was nothing like the President of the United States of America. Rebecca had learnt all about him at school, and he wasn't stuck in a garden, hanging from a fence!

Besides, it seemed to her that Miss Bateman was the one in charge, as she did most of the talking. It all seemed a bit strange to Rebecca, but she politely returned his greeting all the same.

"Then there's Star Jasmine," Miss Bateman continued. "She is over there on your right. You should be able to identify her by her delightful perfume."

Rebecca turned, and was amazed by the sweet aroma of the delicate-looking plant with white flowers.

"Hmmm," Rebecca breathed in deeply. "Really beautiful." She was lost for words by the wonderful fragrance in that part of the garden.

"Please, please! Do not inhale so deeply," came a soft but clearly irritated voice. "It makes me shiver!" Rebecca was taken aback by this sudden outburst from Star Jasmine.

"Oh, I am sorry," Rebecca tried to explain, "it was just that you are…. wwwaaarrr…atchoooooo!"Rebecca began to sneeze repeatedly.

"Hanky, please! Hanky, please!" cried Star Jasmine. "Not over my petals! Those germs are no good for my petals!"

"Oh, you need to tread very carefully with Star Jasmine," said Miss Bateman, half embarrassed by Star Jasmine's reception of a potential ally, who could possibly save the garden from a fate of doom. "She can forget her manners at times, and behave like one of those... er... 'divas' I think they're called.

"Auntie Sue sneezed in front of her a few days ago, and blew off some of her beautiful white petals. She hasn't quite recovered from the shock of that, dear," Miss Bateman continued, trying to excuse Star Jasmine's unfortunate manners.

"What, exactly, is a diva?" asked Rebecca. She hadn't heard that word before now, except when one of the new girl popstars misbehaved on television.

"It's a trendy word for a…" Miss Bateman lowered her voice to a mere whisper, "… a spoilt brat, dear!" she finished.

Aha, thought Rebecca, *I have enough of those in my class at school. I think I'll stay away from her, despite her beautiful perfume. Anything for a peaceful life. What an interesting afternoon this is turning out to be!*

Rebecca's contemplations came to an abrupt end, when her eyes focused on a stunning plant with lilac-coloured blossom. It stood tall and slightly withdrawn from the other plants, right at the edge of the flowerbed.

This plant had thick stems that supported the lilac bulbs in full bloom. Rebecca took an instant liking to this flower. There seemed to be something sad about it, though, as it looked isolated.

"Wow!" exclaimed Rebecca, "and who are you?" No reply. Rebecca peered closer at it, and noticed that a small drop of fluid had fallen from its blossom. For a moment, Rebecca wondered if the plant was weeping. Surely flowers and plants did not and could not cry, but then again, until this afternoon she didn't even think they could speak. She decided not to dismiss anything.

"You are beautiful, and I love your colours – they are very princess-like," she said, hoping to coax out a response. Nothing.

"Forget her, she's such a snob!" shouted a loud, high-pitched voice, coming from the centre of the flowerbed. "She thinks she's Madam Superior!"

Rebecca looked over to see another plant in the centre of the flowerbed. It stood one and a half metres tall, with blue-grey leaves and spiky yellow flowers protruding out, almost blocking some of the other plants.

"Hiya! My name is Hedychium Gardnerianum, but my friends call me Ginger," she offered, followed by a tinny, high-pitched giggle. Rebecca warmed to her immediately. She could see that she would be fun to speak with, as she seemed to have a lively and fun-loving manner.

"Her name is Lily – African Lily," she said, referring to the lilac plant Rebecca had been admiring moments earlier. "She's a snob, and doesn't speak to us," Ginger continued.

"Not so, Ginger!" objected Miss Bateman. "She's probably just shy. She's quite new here," Miss Bateman went on to explain. "Auntie Sue went to the nursery yesterday – or was it the Chelsea Flower Show? - and brought her back. It's quite likely she is still feeling a bit homesick. It does take a while to fit in and feel at home here, you know. Give her a chance!"

"Well, I think she is unfriendly and horrid!" said Ginger, ignoring Miss Bateman's explanation.

Ginger was very young and full of beans. She had missed having other younger plants with which she could have a laugh. Though she had always respected Miss Bateman as a mother figure, she longed for a best friend nearer her own age. With the arrival of African Lily, Ginger had thought that they would be friends and enjoy chats well into the late hours of the evening.

Rebecca could sense that Ginger was upset and hurt by Miss Bateman's defence of African Lily. Rebecca was also certain that there was a valid reason for African Lily's silence. It would just be a matter of time before either she or Auntie Sue had got to the root of the matter.

"Well, I think she is lovely and beautiful," stated Rebecca, knowing full well that African Lily would have heard every word.

Chapter Four
RESCUE

"Rebecca!" called Auntie Sue from the kitchen window. "I hope you've done your homework. Supper is ready."

"I've got to go," Rebecca said to the plants. "Thank you, Mr President, for helping me with my maths."

With no time to check the answer, however, she hurriedly scribbled '58' onto her homework sheet. Quickly, she gathered together her elderflower water, book and pencil.

Auntie Sue was lovely, but she

didn't like having to call a second time, so Rebecca knew there was no time to waste. "Well, it's been very nice speaking to you all," she said, as she walked towards the clematis and other flowers, "but I must go for supper, now."

"Do come back and talk to us," requested Miss Bateman.

"And remember… we're at war!" reminded the President.

"Of course!" promised Rebecca, "and I will bring you a drink and some supper, too, if you wish," she added, as she walked towards the house.

"She won't be back, you know. She'll be just like the rest of them, and forget everything she's heard," said the President, "then we'll all perish!"

"Hmmm, I don't think so," said Miss Bateman thoughtfully. "She's different, I can tell. She's very sensible, intelligent and, above all, she's very kind. No, she is definitely not like the rest of them."

"You could be right there, Miss Bateman," agreed Star Jasmine. "She is the only one who hasn't stolen a handful of my petals and leaves for some strange concoction."

"Well, I liked her!" said Ginger.

"Me, too," whispered African Lily, so quietly that no one could hear.

It was now later that day, and Miss Bateman was awoken by fingers rummaging through her leaves and blossoms.

"Oohh, oohh," she said with a start, as she tried to make out what was being said, and who was standing before her.

"There they are!" said Rebecca excitedly. "Look, Auntie, can you see the nibbles? Something has been nibbling at them all."

"Good heavens!" exclaimed Auntie Sue. "You clever girlie. How on

earth did you find those? I will have to treat this tomorrow without fail, or I'll lose all my plants, and we wouldn't want that, would we?" said Auntie Sue, thinking aloud.

"Oh no, Auntie Sue," agreed Rebecca, cringing at the thought. "They are all such lovely plants and flowers, it simply wouldn't be the same if they were not here."

"You're right. Absolutely," Auntie Sue agreed.

Miss Bateman smiled to herself, as she watched the duo make their way back to the house.

"See you soon," she whispered to Rebecca, who she felt might just be able to hear her.

As Miss Bateman fell asleep, she could faintly hear Auntie Sue saying, "… and you did so well with your homework, Rebecca. I've checked your maths, and you got all your sums correct, even the harder ones. Yes, it was 58. You *are* a clever girl!"

Indeed she is, thought Miss Bateman. *Indeed she is*, and she drifted back off to sleep as the night drew in.

Rebecca enjoyed walking in the garden.

Chapter Five
AFRICAN LILY

Rebecca woke up the next morning and hurried downstairs. She found Auntie Sue reading a large, thick book with lots of photos of flowers in it.

"Good morning, Auntie," she said. "What are you reading?"

Auntie Sue had already been to the garden to treat the plants of all the pests that she had found the day before. While she was there, she had also noticed that African Lily did not look very bright at all.

"My African Lily isn't very well," she said, flicking through the pages, "and I'm not too sure why…"

Rebecca remembered that, unlike the other plants, African Lily didn't talk, and looked very unhappy.

"There it is… Agapanthus – African Lily," Auntie read aloud. "Loves sunny position, slow-release fertilisers, best grown in a container… That's it!" she exclaimed. "Poor little thing. The fertiliser was wrong, and she needs to be in a container if she's to stand a good chance of growing well!

"Let's get to work," Auntie continued, turning to Rebecca, who had positioned herself firmly beside her auntie to look through the pages of the book. "Rebecca – bathroom, breakfast, and to work!" Auntie ordered, however, snapping the book shut.

Before long, Auntie Sue had taken out a large, blue, ceramic pot,

placed it onto the lawn, and poured new soil and slow-release fertiliser into it. African Lily was carefully removed from the edge of the flowerbed, where she had been planted beside Ginger. Very gently, Auntie Sue sat her in her new home, the blue pot, and then bedded in the soil around her root ball.

"There!" Auntie said, rising to her feet and dusting herself off. "We'll see how she does after a day or two."

She then went into the kitchen to wash her hands, while Rebecca continued to stare at African Lily, waiting.

"Hello," she said after a long while. *Will she speak?* Rebecca wondered.

"And a big Hello to you, too!" African Lily had spoken. Rebecca was so surprised that she nearly fell over!

"I *knew* you could speak!" she said to African Lily, "and I just knew there had to be a reason."

"Well, you *are* a clever girl, aren't you?" African Lily replied, in a huff.

"What's the matter with *you*? Why are you so cross?" asked Rebecca. She could see that African Lily was very grumpy, and couldn't understand why.

"They called me a snob, and all sorts of horrid names," she protested. "How would *they* feel if *they* had been given horrid food, and a horrid edge of a horrid flowerbed?"

African Lily paused, but Rebecca said nothing. She sensed it would be better to keep quiet right now.

"I came from a lovely home, where I had a very pretty pot. And where do I end up?" she started to sob, "Right on the edge of a wilderness!"

"You poor thing," Rebecca sympathised, very sad that African Lily was so upset. "I'm sure they didn't mean anything by it."

"But they should have read the instructions!" African Lily exclaimed. Rebecca agreed with her, but stayed quiet. I'll let her get it off her chest, she decided.

"And that ghastly Ginger!" African Lily continued. "As common as muck! Did she not go to finishing school?"

"Finishing school?" Rebecca asked. She'd never heard of *that* before. She was sure plants didn't go there, though.

"Never you mind!" African Lily snapped. "How dare she call me a snob. It's not my fault that I'm from a royal line."

I think not, Rebecca thought, but continued to listen politely.

"And that horrid Star Jasmine..." African Lily started again.

Within minutes of being re-housed, African Lily did nothing but complain bitterly about the other plants. Rebecca began to wonder whether Auntie Sue should have left well alone – it would certainly have been quieter.

"African Lily, stop!" Rebecca said firmly, after a few more moans. "You should thank the Gardener in the Sky that you are well and healthy now. Not all plants are, you know," she added, thinking of the poor plants poisoned by Auntie Sue's barbecue.

African Lily suddenly went quiet again. She was surprised to hear Rebecca speak so sternly to her.

"I will speak to Ginger about all the unkind things she has said, but you must forgive her or... or..." Rebecca quickly tried to think of any plant's worst nightmare, "... or your leaves will wither and fall!"

Wither and fall! Wither and fall! Those words echoed like a funeral dirge in African Lily's ears. She had seen other plants wither and fall, and she didn't want that to happen to her. After a few moments' silence, African Lily spoke again.

"Miss Bateman is very nice and kind," she said. "I like her."

"Me, too," agreed Rebecca. "All the other plants are very nice, really. They remind me of some of the children in my class. They can be really naughty sometimes, but they're nice when you get to know them."

"I'm feeling much better now," said African Lily. "I've got it all out of my system."

Thank heavens for that! thought Rebecca. "Good," Rebecca said aloud.

After a long silence, African Lily asked, "Rebecca, do you really think I will wither and fall?"

"Oh no," said Rebecca reassuringly. "Not if you're nice. You will blossom, and bloom every year," she added, stroking African Lily's leaves, "but only if you're nice!"

Rebecca was looking at the other plants in the flowerbed, when Auntie Sue re-entered the garden, saying, "I've decided this beautiful pot would look wonderful positioned right *here*." To Rebecca's shock and horror, Auntie had plonked African Lily right next to Ginger.

"Please, Auntie, could you tell me how to look after plants too, so they will blossom just as nicely?" interrupted Rebecca, in a vain attempt to make a swift exit from the Ginger and African Lily saga, which was about to erupt before her very eyes.

"Well, they need a good meal – so the right plant food is important – water and tender loving care," Auntie began, totally oblivious to the tension building in the garden. "Speak nicely to them and they will flower. Look after them well, and they will look after you."

"What do you mean?" Rebecca asked. "How will they 'look after' me?"

"Well, just look at the bright colours," Auntie replied, pointing to the display. "Just smell that beautiful fragrance," she continued, taking a deep breath of Star Jasmine's perfume.

Rebecca silently chuckled to

herself. She imagined how cross Star Jasmine must be, having her petals ruffled like that again. "They are pleasing to the eyes, and pleasing to the nose," said Auntie. "Yes, look after them well, and they will look after you," she concluded.

But that doesn't answer my question, thought Rebecca.

"Ah, but Rebecca," Auntie Sue interrupted suddenly, remembering an important point. "They are not all the same. They are like people: different likes and dislikes, so beware.

"Some of them like the sun, such as these clematis plants, for example," she continued, pointing to Miss Bateman and the President. "Others enjoy the shade…"

"That's just like some of my friends," Rebecca responded. "Some of them love splashing about in the rain, but I prefer the sun. Tell me more, Auntie." She was very curious to discover that plants could be similar to people she knew.

"Why do they have funny names?" she asked, thinking about the President. She didn't dare say anything aloud, though, in case he overheard and got offended.

"Well… there are hundreds and hundreds of plants, all with different names," Auntie explained. "Some long, some short, some funny. Some names are very difficult to pronounce, so most plants are given names that are easier to remember. This one, for example," she said, pointing to Ginger, "is known as Ginger, which is easier to say and remember than Hedychium Gardnerianum."

Both Auntie and Rebecca moved along, laughing at the thought of saying Hedychium Gardnerianum every time. Neither could say it very well at all. Thank goodness Ginger was now out of earshot.

Auntie Sue went back inside the house to continue her work, leaving Rebecca to wander around the rest of the garden. *One day, I'll have a garden just like Auntie Sue's*, she thought. *And I'll sing loudly and talk to them just like she does.*

Suddenly, Rebecca felt a trickle

of rain on her bare arms, and started to run as fast as she could towards the house. She hated the rain, as it made her hair get very tangled and difficult to comb. She threw her hands into the air to cover her hair for protection.

As she hurried inside, she could see Ginger and African Lily side by side in the garden, and wondered what they were saying to each other. They were steadily swaying back and forth, back and forth. *That's strange*, Rebecca thought, *there's no breeze*. She'd have liked to have been a fly on the garden wall for *that* conversation. Then Rebecca remembered. "Auntie," she called, "what's finishing school?"

Auntie Sue removed some of the damaged leaves.

Chapter Six
MISCHIEF IN THE AIR

"There's mischief in the air!" announced Miss Bateman on Sunday afternoon. Rebecca and Auntie Sue had just returned from the morning church service.

Auntie Sue went into the kitchen to prepare lunch, while Rebecca ran upstairs to change out of her Sunday best. Afterwards, she hurried out into the garden to see if the plants were getting better.

Auntie Sue had applied some medicine to the leaves and roots the day before. African Lily had been re-housed and had started speaking. The President was happier, saying, "Enemy action had been averted," whatever that meant. At least everyone was happy, or so Rebecca thought.

Miss Bateman shattered that illusion a few hours later.

"There's mischief in the air!" she repeated, with a sense of urgency.

"Why, what's the matter?" enquired Rebecca. She had learnt to take notice of Miss Bateman's warnings. She was a wise ol' bird, really.

"Enemy attack looms... again!" added the President.

"Oh no, not again!" exclaimed Rebecca. She couldn't believe that even more pests were nibbling at them.

"A different type of enemy, dear," replied Miss Bateman. "I heard them yesterday, early evening. A-planning and a-plotting they were!"

Rebecca didn't usually get impatient, but she now felt something unpleasant was about to unfold.

"Miss Bateman, can you please tell me what is the matter?" she asked, trying to remain as patient as she possibly could.

"Well, it was Saturday evening, and I was finding it hard to get to sleep." Miss Bateman paused, as if to recollect her thoughts. "As you know, dear, I had been snipped and clipped all over for most of the day."

Rebecca recalled how Auntie Sue had removed some of her damaged leaves and flowers.

"Oh yes, I remember," she replied. "Did it hurt at all?"

"Oh no, dear," Miss Bateman reassured her. "It's just like you having your lovely black hair trimmed."

Rebecca considered this for a

while. No, she simply hated having her hair trimmed, as Mum would pull at her hair whilst combing it into sections. It made her hair feel as though it were coming out from her very scalp!

She had lovely thick, black hair, which she sometimes wore in two large bunches with a glass bobble at the ends. That's when Mum didn't have time to plait it. Rebecca usually complained when Mum washed, combed and blow-dried it.

Her dad often threatened to give her a hairstyle like his. This, he said, would put an end to all the tantrums that took place every time. Rebecca, however, didn't like that idea: her dad was bald.

No, Rebecca decided it best not to contradict Miss Bateman, and to let her continue.

"After all the snipping of the clippers and seeing my dear leaves being cleared away – God rest their souls – I tried hard to get to sleep." Miss Bateman's voice became a whisper, "Then I heard them. They stood on the other side of the fence, and started speaking about doing a job... Here... Tonight," she said for emphasis. "There, I've told you, dear! Mischief in the air!"

"But I still don't understand." Rebecca was confused. What job? Surely it isn't 'mischief' to have a job. Dad has a job as a plumber, and even some of the kids in class have a paper round!

"Come, come, dear. These are burglars," said Miss Bateman. "They have it all planned! You see, they know that your Auntie Sue hides her spare key under the front door mat, and..." She paused to allow Rebecca to take it all in.

She knew Rebecca was an intelligent young lady, and didn't

want her to miss a single detail. "They also know that Auntie Sue leaves her bedroom window open in the evenings. Absolute mischief-makers, they are!"

"Yes, and their awful tobacco fumes went all over my flowers, and tainted my perfume!" protested Star Jasmine. She detested anything that detracted from her beauty in any way.

Rebecca was deep in thought. "Oh, how dreadful," was all she could say at this stage. "I'll have to tell Auntie Sue immediately."

She had visions of two strangers running around Auntie Sue's lovely cottage, with a great long shopping list of items to steal. All her lovely pictures and belongings, gathered into a big black sack and loaded into a dirty old van. "I must tell Auntie Sue right away, without any further delay."

"My dear child," said Miss Bateman, realising the alarm in Rebecca's troubled face. "All will be well! Simply tell Auntie Sue to shut up and lock up, and then all will be well."

"Hmmm," was the only response she obtained from Rebecca, who hurried off towards the house, breaking into a sprint as she called back, "I'll see you soon, Miss Bateman!"

"Poor dear," Miss Bateman muttered, sympathising with her little friend. "Did you see her frightened little eyes? She was so upset, poor lamb."

"For goodness sake, cousin!" interrupted the President. "She's a bright, intelligent young thing. Stop molly-coddling her! She'll be fine! Besides," he added, "to be forewarned is to be forearmed!"

"I do hope she'll be okay," agreed Ginger, who had been quietly listening up until now. She wasn't very good in such serious situations; she preferred having a laugh and a joke. Anything else was best left up to Miss Bateman, she decided, wishing the President would do the same.

"Miss Bateman?" called African Lily.

"Yes, dear?" Miss Bateman was

so relieved that African Lily was now talking, and a member of the garden family at last.

"She's left her little pink drawing book on the bench, and next door's cat has just been on it," she said.

"Typical!" exclaimed Star Jasmine. "That stench will do my perfume no good. No good at all!"

*Auntie Sue had an opportunity
to practise her robust singing.*

Chapter Seven
RED-HANDED

"But how do you know this, Rebecca?" questioned Auntie Sue in disbelief. "Surely you can't possibly know for certain."

"But it's true, Auntie," protested Rebecca. Of all the times she needed Auntie to believe and trust her, it was now. "They were discussing it."

"Who were, and who told you that? How do you know for sure?"

In between mouthfuls of roast lamb, Rebecca considered carefully what would be the best reply to give.

She couldn't possibly say: 'Oh, Miss Bateman, the clematis you planted a few summers ago heard and told me in passing', nor could she mention: 'the President, the other clematis you planted', or: 'Star Jasmine, the plant that behaves like a diva, she heard it too'.

No, Rebecca decided this would not do. Auntie Sue would immediately send for Mum, Dad or the local doctor. Worse still, all three. No, she would simply have to find another way to convince her.

"Well, Auntie, they were overheard discussing our house. They know you hide the spare key under the front doormat. They know that you leave your bedroom window open every evening." *There*, Rebecca thought, *that'll do her for starters, and give her something to think about. Why do grown-ups always take such convincing?* she wondered.

Auntie Sue's faced developed gorge-like frown lines. These lines appeared every time she was deep in thought. Mum had always warned Rebecca not to frown like that as, if she did, she would look like Auntie Sue when she was older. Auntie was very pretty, but those lines made her forehead look as though someone had taken a ruler and underlined three times with a thick black marker.

Hmmm, thought Auntie Sue, *she was right about the pests nibbling away at the plants. How else would she have known where I hide my spare key? She couldn't remember telling Rebecca about* that.

"Don't worry about those awful mischief-makers, Auntie Sue," offered Rebecca, in an attempt to provide some comfort to her still-frowning aunt. "All will be well, I'm sure."

Auntie Sue's mouth suddenly rippled into a broad grin, followed by a loud chuckle. "Rebecca, Rebecca, you are funny! Mischief-makers, indeed!" She broke out into a roar of laughter. "How ever did you learn to talk like that? You sound just like... your mother!"

Rebecca felt relieved. The laughter broke the silence, and made her feel less anxious. Maybe Auntie Sue would listen to her after all.

"Now, you go and get ready for the evening service," she added, "and don't worry any more about this." Auntie Sue gave one of her the-matter-is-now-closed looks.

Oh dear, Rebecca thought. She wished she knew what Auntie Sue was planning. Why did grown-ups have to be so secretive all the time?

"Hurry up, Rebecca!" Auntie Sue called out. "And stop worrying!"

The evening service was sheer agony for Rebecca. Auntie seemed

to love it though; it gave her an opportunity to practise her robust singing.

No one seemed to notice whenever she sang an odd-sounding note here, or an off-key note there. She would simply look higher up towards the ceiling, as though she were away in some far-off land.

Tonight, the service seemed to drag on much longer than usual. Rebecca fidgeted in her seat throughout, imagining Auntie Sue's poor cottage being invaded and ransacked.

"Keep still, for goodness sake!" whispered Auntie Sue, poking Rebecca in her ribs. "We'll be leaving soon!"

It still seemed ages before the final Amen was sounded, and, as if on cue, Rebecca jumped to her feet. With Auntie Sue clinging onto her hand, she hurried towards the exit in an attempt to beat the crowd.

"Slow down! Slow down, Rebecca!" cried Auntie Sue. She had never witnessed such impatience in her usually calm, easy-going niece. Something had obviously ruffled her.

As Rebecca and Auntie Sue entered the house, Rebecca started to frantically search around for any signs of mischief, but there were none. She couldn't understand it. *Miss Bateman has never been wrong before, and she seemed so convincing. Never mind – all is well,* she thought, and went up to bed.

Rebecca was so tired that she hadn't noticed that the bedroom windows had been tightly closed and bolted. Neither had she noticed that the spare key under the doormat had been safely tucked away in the kitchen drawer.

"G'night, Auntie," she said, snuggling down under the duvet. In the distance, she thought she heard the telephone and Auntie Sue's voice as she answered the call…

"What? Where? When?" enquired Auntie Sue agitatedly, shocked at the news that was unfolding before her. "Heavens, no!"

There had been an attempted

Mrs Lewis had spotted the two men climbing through the window.

burglary. Mrs Lewis at Number 9 – two doors away – had spotted the two young men climbing through the window of Number 7. She promptly rang the police, and the men were caught red-handed. The family at Number 7 were all understandably upset, but relieved that nothing had been taken, and thankfully no-one had been hurt.

Auntie Sue reflected on the day's events, as she peeped in on Rebecca, who was fast asleep. In fact, she was out like a light.

"All this talk about burglars and mischief has tired her out," she whispered to herself. "I'll tell her about it tomorrow."

Rebecca's parents would be taking her home tomorrow, and Auntie Sue would really miss her. She enjoyed having this bundle of energy around.

"Mischief-makers, indeed!" she

chuckled. She was glad she hadn't let slip who Rebecca had *really* sounded like…

None other than Miss Bateman!

Chapter Eight
THE GRAPEVINE

Breakfast was a silent affair on Monday morning. Normally, the sound of chatter and laughter could be heard, but not this morning. Rebecca was deep in thought about Miss Bateman's talk of burglars. Auntie Sue was also deep in thought about Rebecca's talk of the garden.

"You must make sure you're packed and ready for this afternoon," she reminded Rebecca. "Your parents will be here later."

"Yes, Auntie Sue," Rebecca

replied, and rose from her chair to clear the table.

The half term week with Auntie was finally coming to an end. Rebecca looked out the kitchen window, into the garden. It was only a few days ago that she had met Miss Bateman while trying to do her maths homework. She had enjoyed meeting all the others: the dear President, with his military talk; beautiful Star Jasmine and her diva-like behaviour, whose fragrance reminded her of one of her mother's perfumes.

Then there was Ginger. Rebecca smiled at the thought of mischievous Ginger. She was so like Rebecca's best friend, Lucy. She, too, had ginger-red hair, and was just as mischievous. Rebecca had got into trouble on several occasions because of her antics. And finally, African Lily. Ever since she'd been re-potted, she had perked up nicely. She was talking now, and she and Ginger seemed to be getting on like a house on fire.

Granted, Ginger had a lot of apologising to do beforehand. Now they seemed to do nothing but chatter, and Miss Bateman often had to remind them they needed their beauty sleep. That did the trick.

Yes, Rebecca thought, *this has certainly been an enjoyable few days.* But she still wondered what had happened about the burglary.

"Oh, Rebecca," Auntie Sue said suddenly, "I nearly forgot to tell you what I heard yesterday, after you'd gone to bed: two burglars were caught red-handed trying to get in at Number 7."

Wow! Miss Bateman was right after all! Rebecca thought. "Oh, thank goodness they've been caught, Auntie," she said.

"Yes, just as well we'd locked up and hidden the spare key, as you suggested, Rebecca!" Auntie replied, turning to switch on the kettle. "You came to the rescue yet again. I wonder how you manage it!" she smiled, with a knowing wink. Rebecca blushed, and decided to escape into the garden. *What did she mean by* that?

Outside in the garden, Rebecca rushed up to the plants.

"Miss Bateman!" she called. "I've something to tell you! You'll never believe it. Auntie did just as I said, and…"

"You'll be for the high jump now!" remarked the President. "Adults never like to have children telling them what to do… There'll be trouble!" he added for good measure.

"Ssshhh!" Miss Bateman interrupted. "You're being watched, dear."

Rebecca froze, then turned slowly to see Auntie Sue peering out at her

from the window.

"I'm sure it will be okay," she answered, politely waving at her aunt. "Besides, she told me she speaks to the plants, so I'm sure she wouldn't mind if I did, too."

"She 'speaks to the plants', indeed!" mocked Star Jasmine.

"Well, she treats us like babies!" exclaimed Miss Bateman, "with 'What pretty blooms you are', and 'What a lovely girl you are', etcetera etcetera. There's more to us than that, dear."

"Hear, hear!" agreed the others, as though they were a mini quintet warming up for an evening concerto.

"Well," continued Rebecca, undeterred, "Auntie Sue locked up, and the burglars were caught red-handed!" she gushed.

"Oh, that's old news – we've already heard all about that," interrupted Star Jasmine.

"How could you possibly have heard already?" Rebecca didn't believe her.

"We heard it through the grapevine," chirped Ginger, breaking into song.

"That's our secret intelligence," added the President. "It's better than the local papers!"

"Miss Bateman?!" exclaimed Rebecca in disbelief. Miss Bateman was the wisest of all the plants, surely she would explain everything.

"Well," she began, "if neighbours can gossip over the garden fence, then why can't we? I'm firmly attached to it day and night, so it stands to reason that I'll be among the first to hear anything that's..."

Miss Bateman stopped suddenly. In fact, all the plants stopped chattering.

"Oh no," whispered the President. "She's back again, armed with clippers and a big, black sack!"

Rebecca turned to see Auntie Sue marching towards them, with a determined look on her face.

"What on earth have you been saying to her, dear?" Miss Bateman asked Rebecca, nervously.

Rebecca looked on, stunned and speechless.

"There's mischief in the air," Miss Bateman muttered, and fell silent.

"Rebecca! Up to your room straightaway, and get your things!" said Auntie Sue. "Your parents are here."

Chapter Nine
A BIG SURPRISE

There were plenty of hugs and kisses when Rebecca got back inside the house. Mum and Dad were so happy to see her. Mum went upstairs with her to collect her things. She wanted to hear all about her week with Auntie Sue, but Rebecca said very little. Dad took some bags out to the car.

A few minutes later, everything was packed and stacked neatly in the back of Dad's bottle green Ford Estate car.

It wasn't long before Auntie Sue reappeared. Rebecca's mum and dad chattered away with her, lowering their voices.

Rebecca wondered what had happened in the garden. *I do hope the plants are okay,* she thought.

"Come on, Becky, time to go,"

called Mum.

Suddenly, Rebecca felt very sad, leaving the plants. Would Auntie Sue remember to check the leaves regularly for bugs and pests? Would she know not to speak silly baby talk to them?

"Mum, can I just see the garden one more time before I go, please?" Rebecca pleaded.

"Yes, but be quick!" instructed Dad. Rebecca hurried towards the flowerbed.

"I'm going now, Miss Bateman," she said. But there was no reply.

"Miss Bateman?" Rebecca called. *Why wouldn't she answer?* she wondered. "Mr President, what's happened to Miss Bateman?" she enquired, afraid that something awful had happened to her.

No reply. All the plants were silent. No one said a word. Not even Ginger, who *always* had lots to say.

"Well, I've come to say Goodbye and thanks for a lovely week!" Rebecca continued. She wouldn't allow their silence to stop her from doing the polite thing. "Umm, it's been great speaking to you, and I'll really miss you all," she said to them. Still no reply. Tears started to well up in her

eyes. "G'bye, then." She couldn't say anymore, as she wiped her cheek.

Rebecca was very upset, but also annoyed that no one had even had the courtesy to acknowledge her Goodbye. Slowly, she made her way back into the house.

"Oh, I felt absolutely rotten doing that to her. She's such a dear!" cried Miss Bateman, when Rebecca was out of earshot.

"But a deal's a deal!" replied the President.

"It was such bad manners, ignoring her like that," objected African Lily. "That's not how I was brought up!"

"Oh, it was horrible seeing her cry," Ginger said, beginning to cry herself. "She was so upset!

"Oh NO!" interjected an agitated Star Jasmine. "All this weeping and sniffling does my flowers no goo…"

"SHUT UP, STAR JASMINE!!!" the

other plants shouted.

The journey home was long and quiet.

Rebecca sat in the back, strapped in, but still competing with bags and sacks for space. Mum had been shopping, and had all sorts of groceries in those bags, not to mention Dad's tools from working as a plumber, as well as her own luggage.

Mum and Dad were talking about all sorts of boring grown-up things. Rebecca closed her eyes; she was trying to pretend that she was dozing. Mum wanted to know why her eyes were so red.

Rebecca told a little untruth, and said that the plants had irritated her eyes. *Well,* she thought to herself, *in a way it was true!* They had irritated her. She had never been ignored like that before, and it was so horrid of them to do that to her for no reason at all!

Before long, they were parking in their driveway. Rebecca was relieved and happy to be back home. She would be returning to school in the next few days, and everything would be normal again soon. She would still miss those plants, though.

Mum had ordered a pizza with ham and pineapple topping. Rebecca liked picking off all the pineapple pieces, and set to work as soon as it arrived. She was a bit too eager, and burnt her fingers a bit.

Dad, meanwhile, went back and forth unloading the car. Up to the bedroom, back to the car, into the kitchen, back to the car. Rebecca felt dizzy just watching him, enjoying the pineapple pieces as she watched.

Suddenly, her munching was interrupted by a muffled noise:

"Rebecca! Rebecca!" called an all-too-familiar voice. She jumped

to her feet and moved towards the black bags. "Who's there?" she asked.

Before waiting for an answer, she quickly ripped open one of the black sacks on the kitchen floor. There, before her eyes, stood none other than Miss Bateman in a small terracotta pot.

"Hello, dear!" she said brightly. "The others are here, too."

"Oh!" she exclaimed, as she looked down at her five friends in their small pots: Star Jasmine, Ginger, African Lily, the President and, we mustn't forget, Miss Bateman.

"What a really lovely surprise!" she said to them. "Why didn't you tell me?"

"We were all sworn to secrecy – our 'leaves' were sealed!" said the President. Rebecca smiled.

"We *can* keep a secret you know, dear!" added Miss Bateman, chuckling.

So that's *why they wouldn't speak to me! All for a good cause,* Rebecca thought.

Chapter Ten
THE YOUNG GARDENER

Auntie Sue had taken a cutting from each of the plants in her garden. These were to be planted for Rebecca in a small corner of Mum's garden. She had even tied a little message to each plant with clear instructions, followed by these same words: 'Speak nicely to the plants. If you look after them well, they will look after you.'

Rebecca was so excited and quickly opened a white envelope with her name on it that had been tucked away in the black bag. It was a letter from Auntie Sue:

'Dear Rebecca, as a special treat, I want you to have a beautiful garden like mine, but you must remember that plants are like us: different likes and dislikes - some like the sun, some like the shade, some like lots of water, some do not. Carefully follow my instructions below:

Star Jasmine likes the sun and warm weather, and good nutrition (fertiliser which Mother will help with). Give her a good watering once a week, particularly when it is very hot, as she will be parched. Apart from that, she should be no trouble…'

That's what you *think!* thought Rebecca, recalling how Star Jasmine had grumbled when Rebecca sneezed all over her leaves.

'Ginger needs a lot of space to grow, and will be quite glamorous as she develops…'

'Wow!' mused Rebecca, 'I wonder how Star Jasmine will behave having another rival for beauty in the garden! Thank goodness Miss Bateman will be here to keep the peace!'

'Keep Ginger well watered in the summer, but not so much in the winter!' Auntie Sue's instructions continued. 'Remember how poorly African Lily was? Just keep her well potted and watered, and she will be fine…'

Rebecca peered over at African Lily in her pot and smiled. There was no sign of her leaves withering and falling as African Lily had feared. She had remained on her best behaviour ever since Rebecca had given her that warning.

> 'The President is related to Miss Bateman (from the clematis family). He loves the sun, and your mother must apply a slow-release balance fertiliser for his food or there will be trouble!'

Oh dear! Rebecca remembered how the President always seemed to be announcing some invasion or other, *I'll just have to watch and pray!* she concluded.

> 'And Miss Bateman - like her cousin - copes well with

full sun, and needs slow-release food, but do watch out for bugs, as they do like to nibble at her leaves. If you spot them, tell Mother immediately, so they can be treated. It will spare the garden you know!...But you know all about that, don't you, my dear!

> With love
> Auntie Sue xx'

Rebecca was absolutely overjoyed. She recalled how it seemed only yesterday that she had been called upon to save the garden and now... here were her friends, full of life.

She danced around the kitchen. "I'm going to have a garden just like Auntie Sue's!" she sang, as loudly as she could.

Oh what jubilation at being reunited with her botanical allies, and

the fun and games that lay ahead of them in the weeks and months to come!

SPECIAL
BONUS

REBECCA
and the
Strangest Garden

COLOURING
CORNER

Rebecca loved the garden.

Auntie Sue watches Rebecca.

Rebecca sneezes.

Caught in the rain.

'Oh dear!' thought Auntie Sue.

That naughty cat!

Mum and Dad arrive.

Rebecca was so upset!

The sad journey home.

Rebecca's big surprise.

Reunited with her friends.

Auntie Sue's advice.